# TRAPPED

TRAPPED

# SINKHOLE

# TRAPPED

## TOM GREVE

### DARBY CREEK
MINNEAPOLIS

Darby Creek
An imprint of Lerner Publishing Group, Inc.
241 First Avenue North
Minneapolis, MN 55401 USA

For reading levels and more information, look up this title at www.lernerbooks.com.

Cover and interior images: PHOTOCREO Michal Bednarek/Shutterstock (man falling); Milano M (chapter number background)

Main body text set in Janson Text LT Std.
Typeface provided by Adobe Systems.


**Library of Congress Cataloging-in-Publication Data**

Names: Greve, Tom, author.
Title: Trapped / Tom Greve
Description: Minneapolis : Darby Creek, an imprint of Lerner Publishing Group, Inc., [2023] | Series: Sinkhole | Audience: Ages 11–18 | Audience: Grades 7–9 | Summary: Mario has to finish a school assignment or forfeit participation in the Texas high school football championship, but when he falls into a deep sinkhole, he has a lot more to worry about—especially when it fills up with snakes and the vultures start to circle overhead.
Identifiers: LCCN 2022021435 (print) | LCCN 2022021436 (ebook) | ISBN 9781728475486 (library binding) | ISBN 9781728477954 (paperback) | ISBN 9781728479460 (ebook)
Subjects: LCSH: Teenagers—Juvenile fiction. | Sinkholes—Juvenile fiction. | Survival—Juvenile fiction. | High schools—Juvenile fiction. | Texas—Juvenile fiction. | CYAC: Holes—Fiction. | Survival—Fiction. | High schools—Fiction. | Schools—Fiction.
Classification: LCC PZ7.1.G7429 Tr 2023 (print) | LCC PZ7.1.G7429 (ebook) | DDC 813.6 [Fic]—dc23/eng/20220609

LC record available at https://lccn.loc.gov/2022021435
LC ebook record available at https://lccn.loc.gov/2022021436

Manufactured in the United States of America
1 – TR – 12/15/22

The offensive players huddled. Ten players leaned in around the quarterback, who announced the next play.

"OK," the quarterback said. "We're doing '44 trap.' On one. Ready?"

In unison, every player in the huddle shouted, "Break!"

All eleven players broke the huddle with a collective clap of their hands. They jogged to the line of scrimmage. Football practice was close to wrapping up for the day at Foggy Creek High School. The '44 trap' was the team's most reliable play. When executed properly, a defender is allowed to move freely toward the ball carrier for a few steps before getting blocked unexpectedly, or "trapped," before he can make the tackle.

Once in position, every player on the field was still for just a second, poised for action. Then the quarterback shouted, "Ready . . . Set . . . Hut!"

The snap of the ball set off a collision of padded bodies. There were quick movements by runners, blockers, and defenders. The quarterback spun, tossing the ball to a running back who sprinted toward the sideline. Then he turned sharply upfield toward the goal line. The sound of grunts and popping pads could be heard as the runner broke through one tackler. But he was pushed out of bounds just short of the goal line. Once the play ended, other players ran over to help the runner get back on his feet. A long, shrill blast of the coach's whistle stopped the action. Practice was over.

"Nice work, defense!" Coach Crain

Crawford said, his teeth still clenching the whistle. "Bring it in!"

The team came together in a semi-circle around the tall, broad-shouldered, balding man. "Alright! Good practice! But we have to get better by Saturday. We've got to be great if we're going to win State! It's that simple!"

The players—sweaty, dirty, and breathing heavily—squinted at their coach in the late afternoon sun.

"Now, hit the showers, hit the books, and hit the sack. In that order!" Coach Crawford gave a final blast of his whistle. In a well-rehearsed routine, the players crowded together. Each player put a hand in the air.

Reggie Tibbs, the team's senior quarterback and captain, shouted out a count. "One, Two, Three!"

The entire team shouted back at him, "Go Creek!"

With the shout, the players all dropped their hands and relaxed. Slowly, they turned to walk the short distance from the field to the locker room. Some chatted as they walked. Others trudged silently toward the school building.

Reggie and his teammate Mario Sosa, another senior, always walked back together. They were standout players and best friends with a long history. First, as classmates playing catch on the Foggy Creek Elementary School playground, and now as high school varsity teammates. Mario, fast, compact, and strong, was the team's primary running back. Reggie, taller and thinner, was the quarterback.

"I can't believe I got shoved out of bounds when we ran that last play," Mario said to Reggie. "I thought I was scoring for sure."

Mario was a Mexican American teen that had a habit of thinking any play that didn't result in a touchdown was a personal failure. Sports were big in his family, especially soccer, basketball, and football. Mario played all the sports but his passion was for football. He thought about it all year long. When practiced started in the hot Texas summers, Mario was the first one on the field.

Reggie loved sports, but he also had

interests and goals beyond football. A Black teenager with an easy-going personality, Reggie was a natural-born leader.

"It's cool," Reggie assured Mario. You've scored on those trap plays plenty of times. I wouldn't worry about it."

"Yeah. I know. But I hate when I get tackled that close to the goal line," Mario huffed, still thinking about the last play of practice.

Mario and Reggie were two minds with a single purpose: winning the Texas State Football Championship. They'd spent countless days practicing under the hot sun. They lifted weights in the smelly, cinder block weight room at Foggy Creek High. Most importantly, they'd spent many days and nights talking about their team. They planned how they would one day win a state championship. Now, with all that work and wonder behind them, the boys had helped Foggy Creek advance through the state playoffs. Their long-awaited championship dream was just four days away from becoming reality.

"If we run that same trap play on Saturday," Mario vowed, "I'll score."

"No doubt, bro," Reggie said. They walked to their separate lockers to change out of their practice gear.

Foggy Creek, Texas, is a small town on a seemingly endless, arid plain. The shape of the world around Foggy Creek is wide and flat. No matter where a person stands, the view in every direction features only ground and sky, split by the horizon.

In many spots, oil rigs are the only objects breaking that horizon. The rigs rise above the line, separating earth and sky, only to plunge downward, pumping up oil from underground. It's stark but beautiful in its own way, especially in the evening when the setting sun paints the sky pink and purple. The ground darkens to brown and then black.

For Mario, despite being a well-known senior with many friends and a healthy social life, he breathed football morning, noon, and night. He even saw the world as a football field. To his naked eye, the ground and sky would often seem to compete against each other. The horizon line would appear like a skinny referee, separating two enormous opponents.

Reggie thought about football a lot too. But he also had a job and took honors classes. Now that they were seniors, he'd begun thinking about life after high school.

Reggie worked for Mr. Buddy Nguyen. Mr. Nguyen owned a construction company called Win Construction. He told Reggie he chose that name because "win" is how his last name is pronounced. Mr. Nguyen always figured it was an easy name to remember. Reggie liked his boss, and the two liked to joke that they had a "Nguyen-Win" relationship.

Mr. Nguyen allowed Reggie to work around his commitment to football. That commitment was about to be more important than ever in the championship game. Reggie, his teammates, and seemingly the entire school had a single focus of winning the championship on Saturday. Nothing else seemed to matter. Reggie organized the remainder of the week in his mind. There would be three school days, three practices, and three sleeps between now and the championship on Saturday.

Wednesday was the first of those school days. As classes let out as usual at three o'clock, Reggie grabbed what he needed from his locker and headed to practice. The first person he saw was Mario waiting outside the locker room door. Mario silently motioned for Reggie to meet him out in the hallway, away from the parade of teammates making their way through the glass doors.

"Dude, I have bad news," Mario said in a hushed but urgent tone. "McCready says if I don't turn in an extra credit assignment by the end of school Friday, she's giving me an 'F.'"

An 'F' would mean Mario would have to

sit out the championship game. Both boys knew this was no bluff. Mary Ann McCready was known as the drill sergeant of English Literature at Foggy Creek High for a reason. She'd gained the reputation among students as a tough but fair teacher during her forty years of teaching. Mario, despite having a knack for running around and past tacklers on the football field, had now run smack-dab into serious trouble in English class.

"What did you do? Skip class?" Reggie asked.

"I forgot to hand in two writing assignments about Shakespeare's comedies after we won that last game." Mario was referencing the excitement that had surrounded Foggy Creek's playoff victory over Sky View High School the previous weekend.

"Mar-So! Come on! Seriously?" 'Mar-So' was the name Reggie and other teammates had given Mario over the years. It was an abbreviated version of his full name using just the first syllables. As a result, Mario Sosa was known around school by his nickname. Reggie was trying to share in Mario's frustration and be a supportive friend, even though he had warned his buddy not to blow off homework this close to the championship game.

"Yeah. Can you believe it?"

"She couldn't cut you some slack this close to the end of the season?" Reggie asked.

They both knew the answer. Mrs. McCready wouldn't let the best player on the Dallas Cowboys off the hook if they owed her an assignment, even if it was an hour before the Super Bowl. Reggie wanted to help Mario. But what could he do when Mario was up against Mrs. McCready?

"You can't miss the game, Mar-So! Can you get it done on time? What does she even want you to do? Is it an essay?"

"I'm supposed to do a three-page creative writing self-discovery exercise. Whatever that means." Mario shrugged. "I've got some study hall time. And I'll have to stay up late, I guess."

Reggie pressed him further. "Does Coach know yet?"

Mario shook his head. "Not yet. I'll tell him after practice."

"You have to get it done. Coach is going to freak out." Reggie knew if Mario could not play, their chances of winning the State Championship would take a major hit.

Mrs. McCready sat at her desk working. She was a tall woman with shoulder-length brown hair she kept in a ponytail. The quiet hours at the end of the school day were when she liked to grade papers.

She paused while looking at the zeros she had typed in her grade spreadsheet next to Mario Sosa's name. As she pushed herself back from her desk, the wheels on the bottom of her desk chair squeaked on the tile floor. She leaned back and sighed. Like most high schools, Foggy Creek High had rules that made participation in sports or other activities dependent upon students passing all of their classes. Mrs. McCready was upset after telling Mario that he had failed to complete a pair of routine homework assignments. As a result, she had no choice but to let him know that he was in jeopardy of missing out on the state championship game.

With a sense of duty, she pulled out her phone to call Coach Crawford. *After all*, she thought to herself as she scrolled her contacts, *the football coach deserves to know he might have to try and win the state championship without his best ball carrier.*

"Hello, Crain?" she asked as a voice on the other end of the call picked up. "I'm sorry to bother you. But I need to give you a little heads-up on Mario Sosa's status for Saturday."

"Alright, Mary Ann," Coach said. "What's going on?"

"Mario is failing my English class. I'm sorry to put you in a bad spot. I know Mario is an important part of the team. I told him if he finishes an extra credit assignment by the end of school Friday, he can still play in the game."

"I appreciate the heads up. School work comes first before football," he said. "I'm going to go ahead and let him keep practicing. He'll have to understand, though, that if he can't hold up his end of the bargain in your class, he won't see the field on Saturday. Does that sound good?"

"Of course. I appreciate the cooperation," she said. "I'll talk to you later."

"You bet, Mary Ann. Goodbye."

That evening, after another spirited practice, Mario and Reggie went their separate ways. Mario needed to have his chat with Coach Crawford before heading home to get started on his homework, the all-important assignment for Mrs. McCready.

Meanwhile, Reggie headed to work over at Win Construction. His work duties included getting equipment cleaned and ready for the morning crews. He worked silently and efficiently for about two hours. Reggie brought an easy focus to pretty much everything he did.

"I'm all done. Is it OK if I head home?" he asked Mr. Nguyen.

"Sure thing, Reggie!" his boss answered. "You coiled up that cable and put it back on the hook, right? They'll need that right off the bat tomorrow."

"It's on the hook," Reggie said.

Reggie admired Mr. Nguyen. Mr. Nguyen started his construction business in Foggy Creek after growing up near Austin, the state capital of Texas. His family had moved to Texas from Vietnam when he was a young child. Now a successful business owner, he was cheerful and easy-going despite his responsibilities. In addition to his construction business, he owned some oil and gas operations.

As a football quarterback, Reggie took notice of his boss's calm demeanor, even when things got really busy. It wasn't busy tonight, but Mr. Nguyen assured him the work he was doing tonight would make tomorrow's job easier for the other workers. Reggie liked knowing that his role was important for the overall operation of the business. He got that same fulfillment from playing quarterback on a successful football team.

The conversation with his boss reminded Reggie of a phrase Coach Crawford loved to shout during practice through the side of his teeth, which were always clenched onto his ever-present whistle.

"Hey, guys! If we fail to plan right for this opponent," Coach Crawford would yell, "we might as well be planning to fail! Am I Right?"

A grin would always stretch the coach's lips whenever he delivered that line, as if he were proud of his own turn-of-phrase. Thinking about his coach's quirks caused Reggie to chuckle. Then, he felt a pat on his back from Mr. Nguyen.

"Have a good night, Reggie," Mr. Nguyen said. "Get your sleep. This is a big week!"

"Thanks," Reggie said as he left.

On his way out the door, Reggie's attention quickly turned to Mario and the classroom trouble that threatened his spot in Saturday's game. Reggie texted Mario to check on his progress. He got no response. So, he called Mario's phone. Again, no answer. "Huh, that's weird," Reggie muttered to himself.

After the short drive home, Reggie made himself something to eat and texted his parents a quick update. They were working late at the hospital that day. Then he did his own homework and went to bed.

While lying in bed, he wondered if Saturday's game would be like he imagined. Would there be a large crowd? Would any college scouts be there? Would Mario even be able to play? The thought of having Mario sit out the big game caused Reggie to worry. But, after a few minutes, he was sound asleep.

After practice, Mario picked up a burger mega meal and drove home, determined to get started on Mrs. McCready's assignment. His parents were a few hours away helping his grandparents do work around their home. They had left that morning, but they would be home Friday night.

To clear his head after eating, he decided to go for a quick evening run. He quickly called his parents before dropping his cell phone on the table. Then he grabbed a water bottle and a hoodie, put them in his backpack with whatever else he had left in it, and took off.

As his feet kept a steady beat along the white line on the side of the highway, he settled into the rhythm of his jog. When cars would approach, he'd veer onto the gravel shoulder. His feet would briefly kick up dust. Mario enjoyed the relative cool of evening runs and the sight of the gorgeous Texas sky at sunset. With his legs and lungs pumping, Mario thought about what he saw. Once again, it looked like the earth was competing against the sky. The thin horizon squeezed between them.

The sky and the ground around Foggy Creek appeared to Mario like football opponents. The sky, Mario imagined, could drop storms and tornadoes down onto the ground. In response, the ground could whip up dust clouds that might partly hide the sky. Mario was always thinking of ways life could imitate football. He sometimes made cereal stick to the milk, coating the sides of his breakfast bowl in the morning. He'd eat all the cereal on the bottom of the bowl, leaving the cereal on the sides and pretend the bowl was a stadium full of fans.

Now, as he ran at twilight, he imagined tumbleweeds were tacklers to be outrun. He also imagined the world itself to be in the shape of a football competition. The sky was the offense, facing off against the ground, which he imagined to be a stout, immovable defense. After about fifteen minutes, he could sense his mind clearing away the stress of his day.

Breaking from his normal route, he veered away from the road and onto a dusty stretch of desert that was unspoiled by fences or oil rigs. With nightfall nearing, Mario thought about the paper he needed to write and about how Mrs. McCready didn't seem to care about the football team's fortunes.

"I'm no writer," he huffed into the open air. "I'm a runner."

He kept running and let his worries about

the assignment fade away. He would deal with it later.

It was nearly dark. After a few hundred yards of off-road running, Mario realized he'd better turn around and get home to start his homework. Before turning, he reached up to wipe sweat from his forehead. At that moment, in the flat expanse of darkening desert, he tumbled. The realization flashed in his mind that he was falling. Not falling to the ground as if he had tripped, but falling as if the ground itself had just disappeared from beneath him. Seconds later, he landed on a sandy gravel slope. The slope was soft. When he landed, he continued to roll downhill for maybe fifteen feet before stopping.

Stunned, he scrambled to his feet and looked around. He took stock of himself. Although he was shocked and a tiny bit panicked after such an unexpected fall, he was not hurt. He shook his hands and brushed dust and dirt off of himself. Looking around, he could see he was inside some sort of small canyon. In the dim light, he could make out the walls of this strange canyon surrounding him. They were reddish-brown, the same color as the desert dirt.

He picked up his backpack, which had fallen off during the tumble. He turned to climb back up and out of the hole. As he scrambled upward, the dirt would give way and spill down the slope beneath his feet. It appeared that the walls around the top of the hole were at least ten feet high and went straight up.

Mario looked around for a few seconds to ponder his fate. He was still breathing heavily from the run and shaken by the fall. But his reality was becoming clear. He was trapped inside a Texas sinkhole.

Finding as smooth a spot as he could on the floor of the sinkhole, he sat down. He calmed himself by speaking out loud. It was somehow comforting to hear the sound of his own voice.

"Dang. I should've brought my phone for a change." Mario was in the habit of leaving his phone behind whenever he went out for a run. It was the one time he liked to be left alone.

He pulled his hoodie out of his backpack and put it on. It felt warm. Gradually, his nerves calmed after his unexpected tumble.

Using his backpack as a makeshift pillow, he laid back and looked at the stars. After a while, he fell asleep.

Mario opened his eyes to see the faint morning sunlight coming over the edge of the sinkhole. He studied the walls around the top of his sunken prison. They offered no escape route without a tall ladder, which he did not have. It occurred to Mario that it was as if the sinkhole had been designed to trap someone inside.

He had managed to get some sleep, despite hearing coyotes barking throughout the night. He told himself that coyotes rarely attacked humans and, besides, they probably had better instincts than he did so they wouldn't fall into a gigantic sinkhole. *Just my luck this week*, he thought.

"I'm only like a mile and a half from home. No big deal," he said, trying to remain calm.

With the rising sunlight, he began to get his bearings. He could see the sinkhole was about the size of a football field. The floor of the hole sloped downward like a giant funnel to the deepest part right in the middle. At the bottom of the sinkhole was a pond filled with brownish water.

"Great. I can go for a swim," he joked to himself. He took stock of his backpack. There was his water bottle. The not-good news for Mario was there wasn't much else in the backpack that was going to help him. He had a few small pieces of scrap paper, a couple of pens, and a half-eaten bag of chocolate-covered peanuts.

He took a small drink from the water bottle. But he didn't take too much since he wasn't sure how long he might need to make it last.

Knowing it was a long shot, he yelled out.

Someone might be within earshot. "Hello! Anybody? Help! I can't get out of this hole!"

His words bounced around the sinkhole and echoed back to him. He stood still to listen for a reply. There was none. He inhaled deeply through his nose and exhaled loudly through his mouth as he tried to come to grips with his situation.

Mario was vaguely aware of sinkholes in this part of the world. West Texas had earned a bit of a reputation from similar holes developing without warning not far away in a town called Wink. The "Wink Sinks," as they were known, were a pair of huge deep holes that appeared literally out of nowhere several decades ago. The flat, dry ground near Wink, similar in every way to the ground near Foggy Creek, just collapsed all of a sudden. Where there was once flat desert, there are now two massive, deep holes bigger than football fields. They were more than one hundred feet deep.

Occasionally, the Wink Sinks grow larger when a piece of ground along the edge falls into the hole. Mario could only assume that the hole he'd fallen into was a similar phenomenon to the infamous Wink Sinks. But that knowledge gave him no comfort, no peace of mind, and no help in escaping his trap.

Mario had heard theories about what could cause the ground to sink away. He also had an intuition that the sinkhole might just be the result of the football game he'd been imagining between the ground and the sky.

Then he was distracted by the sight of something overhead. In the slowly brightening sky, he could see birds circling overhead. They were not doves or pigeons or anything he recognized as being harmless. These were raptors circling above. They were scavengers looking for dead animals.

A terrible thought crossed Mario's mind. Are these birds waiting to come attack him like he was a meal?

"Do they know something about this weird sinkhole that I don't?"

Mario's football instincts kicked in. He felt he needed to move quickly away from danger, so he hurried up the slope of the hole until he reached the vertical wall. He started looking in the dirt for sharp rocks or anything that he could use as a makeshift shovel. He wanted to try and carve out a little space at the bottom of the sinkhole's wall where he could protect himself from the hot midday sun. That sun would soon be above him.

Mario also thought it might be a good idea to keep himself hidden from the troublesome raptors overhead. As he inspected a larger flat stone about the size of a dollar bill, he felt a pang of worry. He remembered Saturday's championship game and his homework commitment for Mrs. McCready.

"If I can't get out of here soon, I'm screwed for Saturday."

Then he started scraping at the bottom of the wall with the rock he'd found. He went to work hallowing out a small section of the wall, just big enough to hide from the raptors and from the brutal West Texas sun.

Reggie arrived at school Thursday morning and went to his locker. His morning routine usually involved swinging by Mario's locker on the way to his first class to chat for a minute. But Mario was not there. Reggie checked his phone. Mario still hadn't responded to his texts since last night.

Going about his day, Reggie expected to either hear from his friend via call or text, or to simply see him when he arrived later that day. After all, Reggie reasoned, his friend may have a good reason for being late to school.

By the time Thursday afternoon's practice rolled around, Reggie was beginning to worry that something was wrong. Mario never appeared in the hall that day between classes. More texts went unanswered. Now, as Reggie dressed for practice, he noticed Mario was a no-show in the locker room as well. He went over and knocked on Coach Crawford's office door.

"Enter at your own risk!" Coach shouted. He always sounded angry, but he was not a mean person. Reggie and Mario liked to say he looked like, acted like, and sounded like a coach.

"Hey, Coach. Have you heard from Mar-So?" Reggie asked. "I didn't see him in school today and now he's ghosting me."

Coach Crawford shook his head. "No. He hasn't called me. I've been looking for him." He didn't look up as he rifled through his filing cabinet. Coach appeared to be trying to locate something. "I was going to ask you where he was. You guys are thick as thieves after all. I wish he'd call one of us to explain why he's not here, and why he wasn't in school, and why he's failing his English class! Ah! There it is!"

Coach pulled his whistle out of the cabinet and held it up to the light that was coming through the window. Reggie didn't need to ask his next question. Clearly, Coach had found out about Mario's dilemma in Mrs. McCready's class.

"Right. I know. But he says he can get an extra credit assignment done to fix that," Reggie said.

"Well, he'd better," Coach Crawford said. "Or his name is mud. Mar-So Mud!" Coach seemed surprised and amused by his own creativity. "Ha! Am I right, Reggie? Mar-So Mud? That's a good one."

"You're right, Coach." Reggie nodded. "I'll see you outside."

With that, Reggie turned and left the coach's office. His mind was already racing beyond football practice and the state championship game. He was troubled by Mario's absence. Nevertheless, he grabbed his helmet and trotted out to the practice field. He knew he had a role to play in his team's push for a championship. He was determined to do his part, even if his best friend was unexpectedly absent. If Mario couldn't come through, Reggie would have to try his ultimate best to get the championship. But he felt a little lost and uncertain without Mario at his side.

Practice was an unfocused mess. By now, they'd all heard about Mario's situation with Mrs. McCready. The guys were upset about it, and it showed in their performance. Reggie fumbled several times. He messed up the snap count more than once. Coach blew his whistle and shouted at them, making them redo most of the play. They ran extra sprints at the end of practice.

Once practice was over, Reggie was on the receiving end of constructive criticism from Coach.

"Tibbs, you got to be better than that," Coach said sternly. "If you play like that on Saturday, we've got no chance."

Reggie nodded, well aware of his poor play during practice. "I know, Coach. I'll get it together," Reggie told him. "Just one of those days, I guess."

Coach turned and started walking away. As a parting remark, he added, "Make sure it's the last one of those!"

Reggie nodded and started walking back toward the locker room. Then he took a detour. He went down another hallway where he found Mrs. McCready's room. After pausing for a second to gather his thoughts, he leaned into the classroom doorway.

"Mrs. McCready, do you have a second?" Reggie asked.

Mrs. McCready was seated at her desk. A few students getting after-school help were seated together at the desks near the center of the room.

"Sure, Reggie," Mrs. McCready said. She looked at his grass-stained practice uniform. "Are you guys ready for the big game on Saturday?"

"Uh, yeah! Um . . . I think we're going

to be ready," Reggie stammered. He was a little surprised at the question since he always figured Mrs. McCready didn't really care about football. *Perhaps he was wrong*, he thought.

"What can I help you with?"

"Uh, well . . . I wondered if you've seen or heard from Mario Sosa."

"Well, he and I had a meeting yesterday. Is there something wrong?" Mrs. McCready asked.

Reggie glanced over his shoulder to make sure the other students could not hear his conversation with Mrs. McCready. He leaned in closer to her.

"Well, I haven't seen him since yesterday. It seems like nobody has seen or heard from him. It's a little weird, you know? And his parents texted me after the school called to tell them he wasn't here." Reggie spoke with hesitation as he pressed on, lowering his voice. "I, um, I just wondered if you had any ideas about it. Um . . . I know he sort of screwed up in your class. You told him he needs to do extra credit to play in the championship."

Mrs. McCready's eyes widened a bit at the question, as if she'd been surprised by Reggie's knowledge of Mario's problem.

"I'm not going to talk to you about Mario's grades in English class. What I can tell you is that if he completes his assigned work, just like any other student, he can still play in the game on Saturday. But it's up to him to meet the requirements."

Reggie sensed the conversation was making Mrs. McCready a little uneasy. "OK," he said with a nod. "I just have to figure out where he is."

"Well, my goodness. I hope everything is fine," Mrs. McCready said. Reggie knew her concern was sincere.

He straightened himself and prepared to leave. "Me too. Thanks for your help."

Reggie went to the locker room to shower and change. When he was finished in the locker room, he needed to get to work at Win Construction. On his way, he detoured again. He drove to Mario's house and knocked on the door.

Nobody answered. The house was dark and silent. Reggie knew Mario's parents were out of town at his grandparent's house until Friday night. Reggie texted Mario's parents an update that he hasn't seen him yet but that he will let them know as soon as he hears anything.

Figuring it was pointless to send Mario more texts or calls, Reggie hustled to work where Mr. Nguyen greeted him in the workshop.

"How was practice?" Mr. Nguyen asked.

"Good, I guess," Reggie responded. "Can I ask you a question?"

Mr. Nguyen nodded.

"Have you ever had a deal where someone just sort of drops out of sight and won't return your texts or calls?"

"Well, sure, especially if it's a client that owes me money," Mr. Nguyen said, laughing at his own joke.

"No, it's not like that."

"Who is it, Reggie?" Mr. Nugent wrinkled his brow with concern.

"It's my friend, Mario Sosa. He's missed

practice and school. I know he's in trouble in one of his classes. It's not like him to ghost me."

Mr. Nguyen pulled out a pen and a yellow legal pad from a drawer nearby. "When was the last time you saw Mario?"

"Yesterday, after practice. Right before I came over here," Reggie said.

"So, twenty-four hours." Mr. Nguyen wrote on the paper. "Did he say where he was going?"

"To his house to start his homework. But there's nobody there at his house. His parents are out of town and he hasn't checked in with them today. They last heard from him sometime after practice yesterday. The only thing I can think of is that he likes to go for runs when he gets stressed out. Maybe he went out jogging and something happened to him. I can't think of where he'd be." Reggie fidgeted. He was slowly realizing something terrible could have happened to Mario.

"Do you feel like we should call the police? Maybe file a missing person's report?" Mr. Nguyen asked.

Reggie sat silently for a second. He was trying to think of reasons that might cause him to miss a day of school while failing to return his best friend's and parents' texts or calls.

"I don't know. There's probably a simple explanation. I don't want to send people into a panic for no good reason." Yet, something didn't feel right in his gut. This was not like Mario at all.

Mr. Nguyen nodded and put down his legal pad. "Have you talked to your parents about this?"

"Not yet," Reggie answered. "They worked last night, so I haven't had a chance."

"Well, I feel like there is no harm in making the police aware of the fact that a high school kid, whose parents are out of town, hasn't been seen or heard from in twenty-four hours." Mr. Nguyen added, "If Mario shows up, we can just call them back and tell them to forget it."

"Alright, that sounds like a plan."

"Also, I have a friend in town from Austin," Mr. Nguyen said. "She's a geologist and a chopper pilot. She does a lot of work for oil and gas companies across the state. We're headed to check out some fields west of here at first light tomorrow. If Mario got lost or something while he was running in the desert and he's still out there, we might spot him from above. You never know. If nothing else, it'll be an extra set of eyes looking for him."

Reggie's mind wandered back to football and the championship game. He wondered how Mario's absence might affect the team. But Mario missing the game wasn't nearly as troubling as the fact that Reggie just couldn't think of where Mario might be at that very moment.

"Reggie?" Mr. Nguyen asked.

"Oh, right. A helicopter. That would be great," he said as he refocused on the conversation.

"She came up today, but she's working with someone else right now," Mr. Nguyen said. "She and I can let you know how it goes. Maybe we'll find some kind of clue as to his whereabouts."

"Thanks," Reggie said. "I wish he'd just show up."

"I hear you. Now, why don't you call the police? Tell them what you know."

Reggie nodded. Then he dialed 9-1-1.

He explained to the dispatcher that nobody had seen Mario Sosa in twenty-four hours. The dispatcher put Reggie through to a detective who took down all the information Reggie could provide. Reggie also gave the detective the phone numbers of Mario's parents.

The detective explained that an officer would head over to Mario's house to begin their search for his whereabouts and call his parents for any more information and to keep them updated on the situation. They'd also check the hospital. Then they would share Mario's information, along with his physical description, with other police departments from the surrounding communities. Reggie provided the police with his number in case they had additional questions or updates about Mario.

Once the call had ended, Mr. Nguyen asked Reggie if he wanted to skip his work shift that day under the circumstances.

"No. I'm alright," Reggie said. "Thanks for convincing me to call the police. I kind of feel better knowing we did that."

"For sure. Like I said, Reggie, even if Mario shows up, and I'm sure he will, the police won't be upset you made that call. It's just the right thing to do."

Reggie turned to walk into the workshop so he could get started on his chores. Like that day's practice, Reggie performed his work absent-mindedly. He and Mario text each other ten to fifteen times per day. It was truly out of character for his best friend to just go dark without a warning. Reggie carried his worry with him through the rest of his time at work.

Reggie was finishing up his chores when Mr. Nguyen came out of his office.

"You about done, Reggie?" he shouted across the workshop.

"Yes, sir. All done," Reggie said.

Mr. Nguyen kept walking toward him until he didn't have to shout.

"Good. Listen, Reggie, I don't want you to dwell on this too much. As you said before, I'm sure there's a reasonable explanation for where Mario might be. I will talk to my geologist friend, Anna Crude, to see about us taking a quick flyover west of town tomorrow in her helicopter. In the meantime, you go home. Try to get some sleep. If we don't see any sign of him in the morning, we will at least have the peace of mind in knowing the police are also looking for him. OK?"

"OK. Thanks," Reggie said. "I'll see you later."

As Reggie drove home, he yawned and felt himself getting sleepy. He wondered how he could feel sleepy amid his worries about Mario and his anticipation of Saturday's championship game. Maybe he was sleepy *because* of his worries and anticipation.

Just then, he noticed a huge foreboding storm front looming in the sky west of town. This was the kind of storm the Texas plains were known for. It was a storm you could see even when it was many miles away. The flat land with few trees left no place for the storm to hide. Reggie could sense this storm was moving very quickly.

As he approached his house, the clouds burst. Heavy, fat raindrops pounded down onto the roof of his car. He turned the wipers on as fast as they could go so he could see. Driving slowly in the downpour, Reggie pulled into his driveway. A lightning flash lit up the front of his house for a split second, making it appear as if it were high noon. Then the dim light of dusk returned as the rain kept hammering the car. He pulled into the garage and closed the door. Once inside, the sound of the rain changed. The muffled impact of raindrops became a sharper, more violent sound.

It was hailing now. In the fading evening light, the white pellets looked like millions of golf balls falling and bouncing off the ground. For a few seconds, Reggie couldn't tell if the hail was falling from the sky or shooting up from out of the earth. It was coming down that hard and fast. He shook his head to try and toss the surreal vision out of his mind. He sat down heavily onto the couch, feeling himself sink into the cushions.

The noisy pelting of hail on the roof continued. Reggie felt weighted down with worry about Mario. His eyes got heavy. A troublesome, helpless feeling blanketed him.

He tried to reason with himself. Maybe Mario is seeing a cousin he's never told him about. Maybe he's just staying with another relative and simply forgot to tell his best friend. Maybe he's actually fine and simply lost his phone.

Suddenly, sirens blared outside the window. Reggie jumped up and ran to the window. Flashing police lights sped past the house. It was now dark, and the hail was still coming down. In a brilliant, prolonged flash of lightning, the entire scene outside the window was flooded with white light. Night turned into strobing daylight.

In the flashes, Reggie saw the strangest thing he could possibly imagine. The ground appeared to be moving or vibrating. He squinted to focus his eyes. Leaning in close enough for his breath to fog up the windowpane, he saw a carpet of snakes covering the ground. There were thousands of them. All of them black. All slithering frantically in every direction.

Lightning crashed again. A massive thunderclap shook the house. The storm was directly overhead. Another flash delivered the strangest thing Reggie had ever experienced. Hundreds of raptors started landing amid the sea of snakes, plucking them off the ground. Then the birds flew off with them in their talons. The snakes that were not captured and carried away by the birds kept up their frantic chase on the wet ground. More sirens wailed in the night.

Reggie kept his face pressed up against the window. More raptors savagely ripped the snakes from the ground and flew away with them into the darkness. Chaos reigned. The hard rain kept falling. Reggie watched it all in disbelief.

He went into the garage to find a flashlight, thinking he might go outside and investigate. His focus changed quickly once he turned on the garage light. A single black snake was squeezing itself under the garage door, trying to get inside. Like many garage doors, the seal between the closed door and the floor of Reggie's garage was not air-tight—smaller snakes could slither underneath.

Reggie reacted fast. Grabbing a flat-ended shovel, he banged the cement floor just inches from the snake, causing it to retreat back under the door. Immediately, another snake appeared under the opposite end of the door. Within seconds, Reggie found himself in a frantic game of whack-a-snake. He sprinted back and forth, repelling the snakes out of the garage. He didn't have to hit the snakes or kill them. Simply slamming the shovel onto the cement seemed to scare them away. He could also hear the impact of raptors landing on the edge of the garage roof, waiting to pounce on the snakes that were being forced back out from under the garage door.

Without stopping, Reggie jumped up and grabbed a large folded blue tarp that was resting on a shelf. Working the shovel in one hand and holding the tarp in the other, he snapped the tarp open. Then he laid it out on the floor in front of him. He began using the shovel to tuck it into the small crack between the ground and bottom of the door. Within a minute, he'd blocked the snakes' access.

Reggie was breathing heavily. He watched along the bottom of the garage door. No more snakes were trying to enter. Satisfied that he'd blocked their path into the garage, he went to the window and looked outside. The rain still fell and the lightning flashed. The snakes still slithered on the grass and in the street. The raptors continued their attacks. Reggie staggered backward, away from the window. He sank back into an old, padded armchair, not fully believing what he was witnessing.

Mario watched the rain run in muddy streams down the slope of the sinkhole. In the distance, he could hear the claps of thunder and faint wail of sirens coming from the direction of Foggy Creek.

"I'm over here!" he yelled. Mario knew nobody could hear him. He wondered if the sirens might be a sign somebody was looking for him. He had eaten the chocolate-covered peanuts he'd found in his backpack and only had a few swallows of water left in his bottle.

His stomach ached and his throat was dry and scratchy.

Mario sat crouched and cross-legged underneath the tiny overhang he had dug out earlier. Now, the same overhang was protecting him from the downpour. He was not comfortable, but he was mostly dry. Just then, a tiny bit of movement on the ground just beyond his feet caught his eye. It was a black snake slithering past him. Startled, he scrambled out from under the overhang to move away from the snake.

He noticed the rain had finally begun to let up. Then he saw more snakes nearby. He tip-toed down the muddy slope. His eyes moved to the wall of the sinkhole next to his little shelter spot. Black snakes began emerging from the dirt where the wall met the sinkhole's downward slope.

More snakes than he could count crawled out of the ground. They slithered their way down the slope toward the pond at the bottom of the sinkhole. The snakes all writhed around Mario. Some slithered to the right of him, others to the left. It was as if he were standing on an island the size of his bed in a river of snakes.

Mario heard the flapping wings of raptors as they landed on the floor of the sinkhole. With a thud, birds began landing directly on top of the snakes. Soon there were hundreds of raptors. Each one was gripping a snake in its talon and flying off. Every time a raptor dropped out of the sky, the snakes would alter the direction they were moving.

Mario stood frozen. After what felt like an eternity, but was really about five minutes, the snake migration slowly stopped. The raptors remained overhead, but they stopped their diving missions. The chaos eased. Mario tip-toed toward his backpack in his dugout.

He tried to make sense of what he'd just witnessed. The rain, the raptors, and the sinkhole itself all seemed to be part of a strange competition. He realized the same competition he'd thought about earlier, between the ground and the sky, was happening all around him inside the sinkhole. Only now, he was a part of it too.

Was the sinkhole just a spot where the horizon failed to keep the ground and the sky separated? Were the snakes and the birds of prey role players in that competition? They seemed threatening, but neither the snakes, nor the raptors had bothered Mario. It was as if they couldn't see him or had decided he should be left alone.

He thought about the Wink sinkholes and wondered if the same strange scene happens there on occasion. Were sinkholes just strange desert portals? Or was he imagining things because he was dehydrated, hungry, and sleep-deprived?

*The sinkhole was most certainly real,* he thought. If it wasn't real, he would simply run back to Foggy Creek, finish his assignment, and get back to preparing for the game. But he was trapped. There was no denying it.

The storm let up. The only snakes Mario could see were gathered at the pond at the bottom of the hole. Despite Mario's bad luck and crazy misfortune, he was still OK.

Standing there, trapped in a dark sinkhole,

Mario spoke his thoughts out loud. "It's like football. The sky and the ground in the desert are like football teams competing," he said. "Sometimes the ground gets the upper hand. Sometimes it's the sky. Sometimes, when the earth and sky are locked in a fierce battle, a kid might get tackled by a giant sinkhole. This is just how the world works for me out here in the Foggy Creek desert."

The football analogy caused him to think of Saturday's game and his hopes to be a part of it. Then he remembered his essay. His experience and reflection in the sinkhole seemed like the kind of thing that might apply to Mrs. McCready's creative self-discovery essay. *Of all the places to find inspiration for an essay*, he thought.

He went toward the tiny dugout shelter where he'd left his backpack. In the moonlight, visible now through the parting storm clouds, he fumbled for the pen and paper scraps so he could scribble those thoughts onto paper. He needed to remember them for Mrs. McCready. Once he'd finished, he stuffed the pen and paper scraps back into his backpack. He scooted back against the wall of the sinkhole.

"I need to get out of here!" he said as if to inform the universe of his crisis. His words floated into the void of the sinkhole. Mario felt small. Sitting in a massive sinkhole, surrounded by earthen walls, he knew he needed help to get out of this trap. He wished he had someone there with him. He wasn't scared, but he was not in control of any part of his life at the moment. It was a feeling he despised.

He tried to encourage himself. "If I get out of here, I'm going to write about the ground, the sky, and being stuck in this trap. Mrs. McCready might like that. If I get out of here and I get to play in the championship game, I'm going to play like my life depends on it." In his mind, the first part of that sentence repeated on a loop. "If I get out of here. If I get out of here."

The hard rain fell on Foggy Creek. Black snakes choked the town's streets. Raptors crowded people's patios and roofs and attacked the snakes, leaving a huge mess. Foggy Creek residents began to panic. Police responded to 9-1-1 calls as snakes began to breach homes and businesses.

It was an unprecedented situation. Police called the town's volunteer fire department to help direct traffic away from areas overwhelmed by snakes and their attackers from above.

Mr. Nguyen had locked up at Win Construction and was now driving slowly through town. His windshield wipers slapped back and forth. He kept running into roadblocks. In the pouring rain, he was having trouble seeing very far in front of his truck and he was sitting forward in his seat with his face as close to the windshield as his seat belt would allow. He slowly pulled up to a first responder in a bright orange rain poncho. The person was holding a flashlight in each hand.

"What the heck is going on?" Mr. Nguyen asked.

"Police called us out to block these streets," the first responder said. "It's not the rain. It's the snakes. I've never seen anything like it. They're everywhere."

"Any idea where they came from?" Mr. Nguyen had to shout to be heard above the rain.

"No idea. But there are birds flying down to attack. It's like a wildlife war out here!"

"I'm trying to get to the Foggy Rest Motel. Are any streets open?"

"Try Third Street," she advised. "I came over on that. You should be able to get through."

Mr. Nguyen flashed a thumbs-up sign. He closed his window and drove off slowly. His wipers were still cranking full blast. Mr. Nguyen was headed to meet his geologist friend to go over the plan for tomorrow. But at the moment, he was concerned the night's strange events might derail those plans. The rain came down stronger. Because of the heavy rain, it took longer to get to the Foggy Rest than it normally would.

Finally, he pulled into the Foggy Rest parking lot. Through the rain, his headlights illuminated a familiar orange and white helicopter parked in the field at the edge of the hotel's parking lot. He knew the helicopter belonged to Professor Anna Crude, his geologist friend. He'd ridden in that same chopper with her before when they had surveyed potential oil fields together.

Mr. Nguyen parked as close to the motel's main entrance as he could, then sprinted to the lobby door under his umbrella. He had to jump over several snakes on the way.

The manager of the motel was waiting inside the door to let him in. He held a broom in his hand that he was using as a weapon to chase away snakes in case they tried to slither inside when the door opened.

"Hey, Buddy! Watch your step," the manager said as he let Mr. Nguyen inside.

Homer Lodge had managed the Foggy Rest for as long as Mr. Nguyen could remember. Like most longtime residents in Foggy Creek, the two men knew each other. Mr. Lodge was very involved around town. He'd been on the town's school board for years and was an officer in the Foggy Creek Chamber of Commerce.

"Is that your snake swatter?" Mr. Nguyen asked, pointing at Mr. Lodge's broom.

"They've been trying to get inside," Mr. Lodge said. "Can you believe this? Where are they coming from?"

"Underground, I guess. They've closed a bunch of streets."

"Yeah, and I just got a call. The snakes are in the school," Mr. Lodge said. "Probably going to have to call off school tomorrow."

Mr. Nguyen thought of Reggie and the football team. If school is canceled, would they have to postpone the championship game? The snake crisis threatened to shut the town down.

"Good to see you, Buddy!" a woman said as she entered the lobby from inside the motel. "Seems like I picked the wrong time to visit Foggy Creek."

It was Professor Anna Crude. Mr. Nguyen turned to greet her. He introduced her to Homer Lodge. The three of them stood near the door, looking out at the parking lot.

"Anna, what in the world is going on here?" Mr. Nguyen asked. He thought the professor might offer up an explanation.

"I've never seen anything like it," she said. "I'm a geologist, not a wildlife expert. But clearly, something has upset the order of things around here."

Mr. Lodge spoke up. "I'm sure the rain washed out a few snake dens, but all of them? I just can't imagine. Was there an earthquake or something I might have missed?"

"That's possible," Professor Crude said. "There's a lot of oil drilling going on in this area after all. But I think we'd have felt it. Anyway, it looks like it's letting up." She motioned toward the parking lot. They could see through the glass door that the rain had slowed down. There were no snakes visible under the security lights. The raptors seemed to have cleared out as well.

The motel's phone rang behind the counter. Mr. Lodge turned to go answer it. Mr. Nguyen and Professor Crude moved away from the door and sat at a table.

"Listen, Anna, I want to ask a favor," Mr. Nguyen said. "If we can still fly tomorrow, I promised someone we'd buzz over an area west of town. Strange deal, one of my high school workers hasn't seen his friend since yesterday. He says the friend, a kid named Mario, goes for runs out that way pretty regularly. I told my guy Reggie that we'd take a quick look for any signs of trouble. You know, in case he got lost or something."

"OK, Buddy. It's on the way to where we wanted to scout anyway. It's fine by me. By the way, has he called the police?"

Mr. Nguyen nodded. "Yes. He filed a missing person report with them a few hours ago. But with these storms and all this craziness going on, I'm guessing the police have their hands full and may not make much headway looking for Mario tonight."

"I'm afraid you may be right," Professor Crude said.

Mr. Lodge came back out from behind the counter. "Just heard from the School Superintendent and the Police Chief. Sounds like the worst of it's over. But school's going to have to start late, like around noon tomorrow. There's a bunch of snakes they've got to clear out of the school."

"Start at noon?" Mr. Nguyen repeated. "Anna, do you think we could bring Reggie with us tomorrow?"

"I've already billed you for the chopper fuel," she answered with a grin. "It's fine by me."

"I'll call him in the morning," Mr. Nguyen said. "We can just drop him back in town before we go do our work. I just really want to help figure this out. I can tell it's weighing on Reggie."

"I understand," Professor Crude said. We can certainly cover more ground quickly from the air. Perhaps you could tell the police where we've searched after we're done."

"Good idea," Mr. Nguyen replied. "There has to be an explanation as to where this kid might be."

Reggie's phone rang. He wrestled his phone out of his jeans pocket and saw it was Mr. Nguyen calling.

"Hello?"

"Reggie, did you hear?" Mr. Nguyen asked. "They're delaying the start of school until noon. Do you want to join us in the helicopter?"

"Huh? Why is school delayed?" Reggie yawned as he looked outside. The morning sun was shining and the sky was blue. It was taking Reggie's mind a few minutes to catch up. He was still wondering why he slept in the chair instead of his bed.

"The storm overnight has something to do with all the snakes everywhere." Mr. Nguyen explained. "I guess they got inside the school. They must have been trying to hide from those crazy birds that were after them."

Now Reggie's mind began recalling the strange events he'd witnessed the previous night during the storm. "When are you going up in the helicopter?"

"Right now," Mr. Nguyen said. "I'll pick you up in ten minutes."

"I'll be ready. See you in a few minutes."

Reggie turned on the TV while he brushed his teeth and texted his parents to tell them why his car was there and he wasn't. Then he told Mario's parents he was going to look for him. Mario's parents texted back right away, saying they were on their way home to help look.

As Reggie was about to leave the house, he was stunned to hear a morning news reporter speaking live from Foggy Creek.

"Police aren't certain why so many snakes emerged from underground amidst last night's storm," the reporter explained. "They say crews are nearly done removing them from the school building. We'll have more on this breaking news situation coming up in our next half hour."

Reggie stared at the TV screen until he heard Mr. Nguyen's truck horn in the driveway. He clicked off the TV and ran outside to join his boss.

"Good morning, Reggie. You get any sleep?"

Reggie shook his head. "Did you see the news reporters are here about the snakes and the storm?"

"Yeah. Saw their trucks," Mr. Nguyen said. "Let me tell you, I think I drove through the worst of it last night."

"I saw the snakes and the raptors. It was nuts!" Reggie said, wide-eyed. "The snakes were trying to get into my garage and I could hear the raptors on the roof! They were swooping down and attacking the snakes!"

Mr. Nguyen pointed to the sky west of town. "Speaking of which, I think they're still hanging around. Aren't those raptors?"

"Yeah, I think so." Reggie squinted to see the birds circling in the distance.

The raptors seemed to move in formation, like a football play being executed by birds. It caused Reggie to feel a new pang of worry. It was Friday morning after all. The championship game was tomorrow. Now Mario's disappearance was threatening the game itself. Could they even play the game if Mario was missing?

Reggie's mind swirled with thoughts. He couldn't stop thinking about Mario, the championship game, and the strange weather happening in town. While he was still lost in thought, they pulled up to the Foggy Rest. The white and orange helicopter was parked in the field at the far end of the parking lot. Its blades were already swirling furiously.

"There's Anna." Mr. Nguyen pointed to the professor seated in the helicopter.

She was wearing the noise-canceling

headphones that chopper pilots wear when in flight. She waved once she saw them. Reggie and Mr. Nguyen crouched down and approached the open door of the chopper. They both clutched their baseball hats so the propeller blades wouldn't blow them away.

Mr. Nguyen sat in front and Reggie sat in the back. They also put on headphones so they could all communicate.

"Anna, thanks again for doing this," Mr. Nguyen said.

"Of course, Buddy. This must be Reggie?" she asked as she turned around to acknowledge her passenger.

"Yes, ma'am. Reggie Tibbs," he responded. "It's nice to meet you."

"Likewise. I'm Professor Anna Crude," she said as they shook hands. "Buddy told me we're looking for signs of your friend who you think might've run into trouble?"

"That's right," Reggie said. "I haven't seen or heard from him in two days. Nobody has. It's weird, and now there's all this crazy stuff going on."

They all spoke more loudly than they would in normal conversation because of the headphones and the chopper noise.

The professor nodded as she turned back to face the helicopter's controls. "Well, let's go take a look," she said.

Reggie buckled his seat belt and felt the helicopter lift gently off the ground and climb upward, a raptor in flight.

Mario barely slept in his earthen dugout at the base of the sinkhole wall. He wondered if he could really trust his eyes in the bright morning light. The only things left in his backpack were his pen and the scribbled notes he jotted down for Mrs. McCready's assignment. He pulled them out to inspect the message he'd written in the dark.

*It's like football. The sky and the ground in the desert are like football teams competing. Sometimes the ground gets the upper hand. Sometimes it's the sky. Sometimes, when the earth and sky are locked in a fierce battle, a kid might get tackled by a giant sinkhole. This is just how the world works for me out here in the Foggy Creek desert.*

Mario thought of the sirens he'd heard during the storm. He held out faint hope they were a sign somebody was looking for him. He needed help soon if he had any shot at getting his affairs straight and playing in the game. Or even getting out alive. He looked up again. The raptors were still circling.

He stood up and grabbed a small stone from the slope. He threw it into the sky toward the birds.

"What do you want?" he shouted angrily in the direction of the circling raptors. "Why don't you fly into town to find me some help or else get lost? I'm sick of looking at you!"

Just then several dozen raptors swooped down into the sinkhole toward Mario. He dove back toward the wall of the sinkhole, but it soon became clear the raptors were not diving at him. Instead, they dove to the water at the bottom of the sinkhole. Hundreds of snakes had re-emerged near the water's edge.

One by one, the birds dive-bombed the snakes, snatching them from the shallow water with their talons and flying off with them. Some of the raptors lost their grip on the snakes as they flew away. It was literally raining snakes in the sinkhole.

Realizing the raptors weren't coming after him, Mario threw a fist full of gravel towards the action at the bottom of the sinkhole. The birds scattered briefly, but they quickly returned. The snakes kept slithering around near the water's edge. The scene, which had filled him with an uneasy dread the night before, now made him angry.

Hungry, tired, and growing desperate, Mario kept throwing the gravel, one fist-full after another. He shouted curses at the raptors and the snakes and the sinkhole itself. He was losing hope of getting out of his trap in time to play in the championship football game. Worse, he started wondering if he was going to die in the sinkhole.

Up in the sky, racing over the town of

Foggy Creek, Professor Crude, Mr. Nguyen, and Reggie scanned the ground from inside the helicopter. Reggie pointed out the TV news trucks. Then he pointed out the football field and Foggy Creek High. He'd never been in a helicopter before.

Reggie glanced west and shouted, "Look! There are the raptors we saw. Should we check that out?"

After living in the desert, Reggie knew that birds of prey circling a location such as this could indicate a wounded person or animal on the ground. Birds of prey are often waiting to move in for an easy meal. It's a brutal reminder of the circle of life.

Professor Crude glanced at Mr. Nguyen. "Sure."

They headed west over a flat, featureless expanse of desert. Then suddenly, they noticed a strange feature take shape on the horizon.

"What the—?" Mr. Nguyen started to exclaim. But he didn't finish the sentence.

Professor Crude finished it for him. "Wow!

That's new. Sinkhole straight ahead. And it's a big one!"

"Looks like the raptors are right above it," Mr. Nguyen pointed out as they drew closer.

Professor Crude flew the helicopter in a circle around the sinkhole so as not to hit any of the raptors in the air. Reggie sat up straight, craning his neck to see down into the hole. Then Professor Crude lowered the helicopter. Reggie saw a brown pond of water at the bottom of the sinkhole. Some of the raptors were near the water's edge. His eyes moved from the pond up to the edge of the sinkhole, where he encountered an even stranger sight.

A person, a young man perhaps, appeared to be throwing things at the birds. The person looked up when the helicopter came over the edge of the sinkhole. Then the person started waving wildly, jumping up and down. Reggie noticed the person was wearing what looked like a gray Foggy Creek High School football hoody.

Reggie's mouth and eyes opened wide.

"I see him! It's Mario! He's trapped in the sinkhole!"

"Hey! Help! I'm down here!" Mario yelled at the helicopter. He kept jumping up and down.

The helicopter slowly and loudly descended toward the sloping floor of the sinkhole. The spinning blades scared the raptors back into the sky and the snakes slithered back into the pond at the bottom of the hole. Their heads were barely visible above the brown water. As dirt and dust kicked up beneath the blades of the approaching helicopter, Mario shielded his face with his arm.

He'd never seen a helicopter from this close-up before, but his relief at seeing anything other than the inside of a sinkhole was making his heart pound.

"Yes!" he screamed. "I'm here! It's me! I'm trapped! Help!"

Still protecting his face with one arm, he waved his other hand to catch the attention of whoever was inside the helicopter.

"Are you sure that's him?" Mr. Nguyen asked Reggie as they both craned their necks to see the stranded person.

"Totally! That's him!" Mario answered. "That's his football hoody and his backpack. No doubt! I see them every day!"

Professor Crude maneuvered the helicopter downward. Raptors soared upward beyond the helicopter's rotor blade.

"I just need to find a spot away from the wall and away from the water at the bottom there," Professor Crude said. She nodded toward the sinkhole pond. "Look at that! More snakes!"

Reggie saw the dark-colored snakes moving around the edge of the pond. They watched hundreds of snakes disappear into the water.

"They must've come here after the raptors tried eating them last night," Professor Crude said.

With that, the helicopter came to a gentle rest on the sloping sinkhole floor.

"Do you want to just keep it running?" Mr. Nguyen asked her.

She nodded and gave him a silent thumbs-up signal.

Mr. Nguyen turned to Reggie. "Let's go make sure he's OK. Then we can get you guys back to town."

Mr. Nguyen removed his headset and hopped out first, followed by Reggie.

Mario had grabbed his backpack and was already stumbling towards them. Reggie broke into a sprint. Mr. Nguyen trailed behind Reggie.

"Mar-So!" Reggie shouted.

"Reggie! Dude!" The chopper blades were loud enough to force them to yell to hear each other. "How'd you find me out here?"

"We got lucky, man!" Reggie answered as they came together. They both jumped into one another, crashing into each other side-to-side in mid-air. They had done the same thing dozens of times together after successful football plays.

Still shouting, Reggie said, "Mr. Nguyen got the chopper from his professor friend. We didn't know where to look, so we flew over toward this flock of raptors and then we found this." He opened his arms wide and gestured at the massive hole surrounding them.

"And here you are, Mario!" Mr. Nguyen said. "Are you alright?"

"Here I am!" Mario smiled. "Yeah. I'm just tired and hungry and happy to see you guys. I fell in here and got trapped while I was running the other night. Once I fell in, I couldn't climb out. And I left my phone at home."

"I knew it!" Reggie exclaimed, turning to Mr. Nguyen. "Didn't I say the other night that he likes to run out on the edge of town and maybe something happened? But I never figured it would involve something like this!"

"Yeah, well, I didn't figure that either," Mario replied. "I was wondering if anybody was ever going to come looking for me. I heard the sirens, but nobody ever came out this way to look for me until now. Hey, speaking of which, can I catch a ride?"

They all smiled at the question. The play-by-play of Mario's ordeal would have to wait. They jogged back along the slope to the spot where Professor Crude remained in the awaiting helicopter.

Nearing the chopper, they hunched over to stay away from the rotor blades and climbed in. Professor Crude turned around as her newest passenger climbed in and motioned for him to put on a headset for the ride.

"You must be Mario," she said. We're certainly glad to see you. Are you alright?"

Mario adjusted his earphones. "Better now! I've never ridden in a helicopter before. Now I've really seen it all."

The chopper rose from the hole. Mario looked down on what had been his desert prison for the past forty-eight hours.

"So how did you fall in there?" Professor Crude asked.

"It was dark," Mario answered. "I didn't see it until I was in it! It was like it came out of nowhere. I shouldn't have turned into the desert. The sky just looked so awesome . . ." His explanation trailed off.

Mr. Nguyen chimed in. "It did come out of nowhere, you guys. I was out here last month right around this same spot. It was just flat desert. That sinkhole is brand new!"

"I don't get it," Mario said. "Is it like the ones in Wink?"

Professor Crude spoke up as she concentrated on the controls of the chopper. "It's a weird deal. Bedrock underground can give way over time because of water seeping through. If a cavity forms in the eroding rock underground, it can collapse, pulling the ground at the surface down with it. If that happens, ta-dah, sinkhole!"

Mario carefully listened. Professor Crude's calm explanation made sense. He thought it probably makes her good at her job if she can explain things so quickly and easily.

"Huh, I wondered if it might've been the snakes that caused the hole to form," Mario said.

Reggie nodded. "That's right! We saw the snakes in the sinkhole. They were in there with you, too? All night?"

"Yeah. Like a million of them. Those crazy raptors diving for them from the sky."

Mario gestured with his hands to mimic birds aggressively diving downward. "It was freaky!"

"The same thing was happening in town," Reggie explained to Mario.

Mario's brow rose. "Really? I just thought that was part of what goes on inside a sinkhole." He gazed out the helicopter window as if he were scanning the sky for an explanation.

Reggie reached around the seat and tapped Mr. Nguyen on the shoulder. "Do you think the snakes came in to town from the sinkhole when it formed? Maybe last night they decided to try and get back to the sinkhole during the storm."

Mr. Nguyen hunched his shoulders with his palms up. "I have no idea." He looked toward Professor Crude.

"Oh, the snakes?" she said. "Well, there are snakes in the desert, of course. I don't know why so many of them emerged all at once. And in multiple places. That's just freaky. There may well be an explanation, but right now I don't know what it might be."

Mr. Nguyen turned back toward Mario and Reggie. "Hey, I almost forgot. We need to call the police and let them know our guy Mario here is no longer missing. Do you want to do it, Reggie?"

"Sure! I'll call as soon as we're on the ground."

"You guys called the police about me?" Mario asked.

"With all the drama last night and the snakes and all that, I'm not sure they'd gotten too far looking for you just yet," Reggie said. "I talked to your parents too. They have been freaking out and are on their way home."

"Could I borrow your phone to text them quick?" There wouldn't be time to tell them everything. Right now he wouldn't be able to hear them on the helicopter. But at least he could tell them he was OK.

Reggie gave Mario his phone. "Of course."

They flew in silence for a few minutes. Mario recalled his run Wednesday evening under the pink and purple sky that started his whole ordeal. That sky was now perfectly clear in the morning sun.

"Maybe the snakes were agitated because they want to see us win the championship," Reggie said. "Mar-So, you're telling me Foggy Creek's best running back couldn't get himself out of that hole?"

They both grinned. The comment brought their thoughts back to the challenge that remained unsolved. Mario was no longer trapped by the sinkhole, but he still wasn't free to play in the big game.

"I have got to get to school and write up my assignment," Mario said. "But I think I need to eat first."

"Let's go to my house," Reggie said. "Shower and sandwich. In that order." He said it in the same way that Coach does. "You can borrow some clothes. Then we'll head to school. It's starting late today because of the snakes. I guess a few got in the school."

"Seriously?" Mario asked.

"Crazy night, Mar-So," Reggie said. "But I'm stoked we got you back!"

All four occupants in the chopper nodded as they descended into a field to land and let the boys out near Reggie's house.

Clean, fed, and anxious to straighten out his academic predicament as soon as possible, Mario hopped in Reggie's car. The two headed for school.

In the school parking lot, they passed several TV news trucks and camera crews. Reporters were milling about covering the great Foggy Creek snake infestation that had delayed the start of school.

"Are you students? Can we ask you about last night?" one reporter asked.

"Uh, OK," Mario answered.

Reggie wished they had just kept walking. But he stopped with Mario as the reporter and her camera person moved around them to properly record their conversation. The reporter coached Mario to ignore the camera and just talk to her. Then she began her questions. First, she asked Mario to say and spell his name so they could properly identify him on the air.

"Mario Sosa." Then he spelled out his name. "I'm a senior here at Foggy Creek.

"Did you see snakes around town last night?" The reporter tilted the microphone toward Mario.

"Yeah. Like a billion of them. But I wasn't in town. I was trapped in a sinkhole west of town for the past two nights. That's where I saw them."

The reporter paused, clearly confused by Mario's answer. "Wait. You were trapped in a sinkhole and just got out this morning?"

"Crazy deal, huh?" Mario went on with his explanation. "The sinkhole was crawling with snakes. The raptors were diving down from the sky to attack them."

"This all happened in the sinkhole?" the reporter asked. "Then what happened?"

"Well, the raptors were still attacking the snakes this morning when my friend here and his boss and their professor friend found me with a helicopter. Good thing, too, because we're supposed to play in the state title game tomorrow, and I was starting to worry."

"Wait! What kind of a sinkhole are you talking about?" asked the reporter. "You don't mean the ones near Wink, do you?"

"No," Mario answered. "There's a huge sinkhole that just formed maybe two or three miles west of town. The professor says it's probably from the same erosion underground that caused the ones up near Wink. The one I fell into is off the road quite a ways. I sort of found it by accident."

Reggie was listening to the interview and getting impatient. There was work to do, after all, and a championship to win. He spoke up. "Mario, we should go. We have to find Mrs. McCready and Coach Crawford. Remember?"

"Oh, yeah. Sorry. I have to go," Mario said to the reporter.

She shouted after the boys, "Can we get your number? We'd love to know more about your ordeal!"

The boys waved her off and kept walking toward the school.

The reporter turned off her microphone. "I think we need to go find this sinkhole," she told her camera operator. "I'll call the station."

Inside the school, the boys saw the exterminator crews cleaning up their equipment and preparing to leave before classes started. Aside from that, there were no obvious signs that there had been a snake infestation overnight.

The boys split up. Mario headed to his first class, which luckily, was study hall. He would get one period to craft his thoughts for Mrs. McCready's extra credit essay.

Mario pulled out of his backpack the dog-eared notes with his thoughts from the sinkhole. Over the next hour, Mario wrote a three-page essay about self-awareness that emerged for him while he'd been trapped in the sinkhole. He wrote about his tendency to see the world through his own football-centric imagination that turned the endless Texas sky into an offense and the flat desert ground into a defense. He wrote about how the horizon line failed to keep the two sides separated. The snakes, the raptors, the sinkhole, and even Mario himself were all caught up in the scrimmage. His thoughts flowed out as he typed. Finally, he wrote his conclusion:

*The sky and the ground in the desert are like football teams competing. Sometimes the ground gets the upper hand, sometimes it's the sky, and sometimes, when the earth and sky are locked in a fierce battle, a kid might wind up trapped in a giant sinkhole. This is just how the world works for us here in the Foggy Creek desert, where our friends always help us out.*

By the time classes ended, the media that had
assembled outside the school had cleared out.
One by one, they'd all gone out west of town
to report on the newly discovered sinkhole.
Thanks to Mario's interview earlier, it was
no longer a secret. Reggie found Mario at his
locker putting his books away.

"Did you finish it?" Reggie asked.

"I emailed it to her after study hall," Mario
answered. "Now I'm headed over there to talk
to her."

"Good luck, Mar-So! I'll see you at practice.

Mario walked down the hall and knocked on Mrs. McCready's door.

"Come in, Mario. Have a seat," she said.

Mario moved nervously toward the chair next to Mrs. McCready's desk and sat down.

"Mario, let me just say how glad I am to know you're OK. Your friend Reggie was worried about you. And so was I."

"Thank you."

Mrs. McCready continued. "I can tell from what you've written here that you put some thought into the exercise. Mostly, I'm satisfied that you tried to express some of your own self-awareness. I'm just sorry you had to be trapped in a sinkhole for as long as you were."

"Yeah, well, I guess I shouldn't run in the desert after dark," Mario joked. "That's probably a good bit of self-discovery."

Mrs. McCready laughed. "Well, yes. I won't argue with that assessment. Now, you better get to practice. I happen to know Coach Crawford hates it when his players are late. I'll just say, let's not miss any more assignments.

And let's go win a Texas State Championship this weekend!"

"Thank you!" Mario said. He jumped up with a combination of joy and relief and ran for the locker room.

Mario dressed quickly for practice and joined the team near Coach Crawford's office, where Coach had his TV tuned into the local news. The players gathered around. Mario moved in next to Reggie and gave him a high-five to let Reggie know that he'd gotten the green light from Mrs. McCready.

On TV, the same reporter Mario had spoken to earlier that day now stood on the edge of the sinkhole where Mario had been trapped until that morning.

"The sinkhole formed just west of the town of Foggy Creek," she said as the camera panned across the sunken landscape. "The town found itself overrun by snakes last night." The reporter continued in dramatic tones. "We're now joined by Professor Anna Crude, a geologist from the University of Texas.

Professor Crude, do you think the snakes had anything to do with the formation of this new sinkhole?"

Mario and Reggie shared a knowing glance. Mario, having thought about and written about his sinkhole experience to complete his essay, didn't care to rehash the ordeal at that very moment with his entire team.

As Professor Crude spoke to the reporter about the various natural forces at work in the formation of sinkholes, the boys turned to head out to the final practice of their high school careers.

For the next hour and a half, they worked on preparing for the big game that was now just a day away. Mario, despite feeling the fatigue of someone who hadn't had a good night's sleep in nearly seventy-two hours, managed to have a strong practice. His running was strong, he made several impressive blocks, and in general he played with focus and determination. As practice wound down, Coach Crawford led the team through their end-of-the-day routine.

Coach blew his whistle. "Alright bring it in!" he yelled.

The team stood in their customary huddle around the coach.

"Listen up!" Coach yelled. "Our bus leaves from school at ten o'clock. This is a business trip, guys. Our business is a state championship. We've got to have everybody keep their nose clean tonight and tomorrow." He looked directly at Mario and paused briefly before continuing. "Now, hit the showers, hit the books, and hit the sack, in that order!" The coach gave a final, long blast of his whistle.

The players crowded together. Each player put a hand in the air.

Reggie shouted out his count, "One, Two, Three!"

In unison, the entire team shouted back, "Go Creek!"

By Saturday morning, life had practically returned to normal around Foggy Creek, except for the fact that a massive sinkhole was now sitting like a scar on the desert. The TV news crews did Friday night reports on the formation of the newest west Texas sinkhole and then left town. The term "Foggy Creek Canyon" was being used as a name for the sinkhole. It seemed destined to join the "Wink Sinks" in west Texas lore.

The snake infestation and the attacking raptors that accompanied them remained a mystery. Theories were posted on social media. Some said the storm flooded the snakes' underground dens and forced them all above ground at once. Others said there'd been an undetected earthquake or that the raptors were spooked by a supersonic airplane from a nearby air force base. None of the theories seemed too far-fetched, and yet, at the same time, none of them really seemed true.

The night before the big game, Mario and Reggie had both slept like logs.

Mr. Nguyen called Reggie in the morning to wish him luck and to tell him he'd seen Mario's interview on the late news as well as Professor Crude's. The professor and her helpful helicopter were on their way back to Austin. But Mr. Nguyen, like so many of Foggy Creek's residents, was headed to Midland, Texas, to watch the championship game.

The team bus headed out right on time at ten o'clock. Mario and Reggie sat together with Mario near the window, as was their custom. It was a superstition of sorts. They'd sat together like this on the bus going to the first game of the season. After winning that game, they decided they should sit the same way until they lost. Since they'd gone undefeated all season, the seating arrangement remained in effect.

After an hour and a half ride, they'd arrived at the field where they'd play for the championship. After getting dressed into their pads and uniforms, Coach Crawford called them together.

"Alright, guys," he began. "We've put in a lot of work to get here. This is a special day for us. We have a good game plan for this game, and guess what, we have not failed to beat any of our opponents this season, and we most definitely are not planning to fail today! Am I right?"

The players shouted back in unison, "Right, Coach!"

"Now, let's go have fun and bring Foggy Creek a state title!"

The game was tense and competitive. Foggy Creek played in front of the biggest crowd the team had ever experienced. Early nerves gave way to spirited competition. Both teams had their moments. Late in the game, with the score tied, Foggy Creek took possession of the ball with a chance to win. As they'd done so many times before, Foggy Creek's offense huddled up so Reggie could announce the next play they would run.

"OK, guys," Reggie instructed, "let's run '44 trap.' On one. Ready!

His teammates shouted back at him, "Break!"

Clapping in unison as they broke the huddle, the offensive players came to the line of scrimmage. Reggie lined up behind the center and called out the signals. "Ready! Set! Hut!"

The words set off a collision of padded bodies and quick movements. Reggie spun, tossing the ball to Mario, who sprinted toward the sideline. Then Mario turned sharply toward the goal line. The sound of grunts and popping pads filled the air as Mario broke through one tackler and found himself in a foot race with three others who were breathing down his neck.

The goal line was ten yards ahead. Mario put his head down. He ran for the corner of the end zone, clutching the ball under his right arm and extending his left arm outward to fend off the pursuing tacklers.

As all three tacklers finally got their hands on him, Mario let out a grunt and dove for the goal line. He stretched out and landed the ball into the end zone, while pulling all three defenders to the ground with him.

The referee blew his whistle, threw his arms skyward, and shouted, "Touchdown!"

The Foggy Creek team swarmed Mario, who was still lying on the ground with the ball. The first player to reach him was Reggie.

"Dude! It's the trap play from practice!" Reggie shouted while joyfully slapping at Mario's shoulder pads. "You predicted this!"

Mario was out of breath. "Bro, I told you I'd score!"

"You did, Mar-So! You really did!"

The offense triumphantly ran back toward

the sideline. The stands on Foggy Creek's side of the field were buzzing with excitement. Coach Crawford gave Mario and Reggie a hug.

The final horn sounded. Foggy Creek had finally captured a Texas State Championship! Mario Sosa, despite a seriously strange week, had scored the winning touchdown on their signature play, the '44 trap,' exactly as he had predicted.

A loud celebration erupted on the field. The players hugged each other and exchanged high fives and fist-bumps. They waved at the cheering crowd.

In the stands, Mr. Nguyen laughed and cheered. Mrs. McCready waved a Foggy Creek flag and yelled with the crowd. Homer Lodge applauded from the top row.

Mario's parents cheered wildly for their son. Reggie's parents were there too, thrilled beyond measure to witness this great moment in their son's life.

Reggie and Mario stood together in triumph. They had overcome a last-minute academic hurdle. They had overcome Mario being trapped in a massive sinkhole. They had overcome large infestations of slithering snakes and dive-bombing raptors. And they had still achieved a Texas State Championship. Nothing could stop them.

Coach Crawford was moving among the players, congratulating them individually.

"Mar-So! Tibbs! You guys are Texas state champs!" Coach shouted, smiling. "Congrats, boys!"

"I can't believe it," Mario said. "Even after everything that happened, we still won!"

Reggie laughed. "You better believe it. We are state champs!"

The celebration carried on in the locker room until eventually, the team got back on the bus. They headed toward Foggy Creek for a celebration pep rally for students and the players' families at the high school.

As the bus rolled along the highway west of town, Mario and Reggie, still all smiles and laughter, paused in their shared seat for a second to notice a small group of raptors flying above the desert. They were directly over the sinkhole that had trapped Mario.

They watched as the birds circled majestically in the pink and purple evening sky before diving down toward the ground.

Mario shook his head. "Next time I go for a run," he told Reggie, "remind me to stay out of the desert."

## ABOUT THE AUTHOR

A self-proclaimed "sports and geography nerd," Tom Greve has been writing broadcast television news and sports content in Chicago since 2007. His TV writing earned him an Emmy award in 2019. He's also written more than a dozen nonfiction children's books along the way, and worked as a network TV producer at the NCAA Men's Basketball Tournament and at Major League Baseball's All-Star Game.

A native of northern Wisconsin, he's lived his entire adult life in the city of Chicago. He is married with two kids. His hobbies include participating in wide-ranging conversations with friends and family, cheering for his favorite college basketball teams, and riding his bicycle.